*Wham!*

Your back slams against the mat after your opponent surprises you with a powerful clothesline to the chest. He's knocked the wind out of you, but you recover quickly. You jump to your feet and then duck to avoid a kick.

You head for the corner turnbuckle, quickly climbing to the top rope.

"You can't run from me, you chicken!" shouts Blockhead, your opponent. He's a big brute, and he's got at least fifty pounds on you. You know you'll never beat him on the mat, so you take to the ropes.

Blockhead charges at you, but you dive off the rope and perform a frog splash. You bring your arms and legs together and then open them wide as you make impact. Blockhead slams into the mat, and you quickly apply all your weight to his shoulders, pinning him down. The ref begins to count.

"One . . . two . . . three!"

*Ding ding ding ding ding!* The bell rings. You're the winner!

Blockhead stands up and grudgingly shakes your hand. You raise your arms in victory and walk around the ring. The crowd in the high school gym begins to clap and cheer. There are only a few hundred people there, but right now you feel like you're in a big arena. This is what it's all about. Sure, you dream of being a WWE Superstar someday. But you'll do the small shows forever if you have to. That's how much you love wrestling.

You climb out of the ring and grab a bottle of water. You want to head home. You've got to wake up early in the morning to train, and you want to be fresh.

A guy in a blue suit approaches you as you're walking across the gym.

"Hey, great match," he says. He hands you a business card. To your surprise, it's got the WWE logo on it!

"Name's Pete. I scout future Superstars for Mr. McMahon," the guy tells you. "How'd you like to audition for him tomorrow?"

"For real?" you ask. It sounds too good to be true.

"For real," Pete assures you. He jots down the info on the back of another card and hands it to you. "See you tomorrow."

You stand there staring at the card for a long time.

It's your big chance! You remember something you saw on *Raw* a few nights ago. Mr. McMahon announced a special tournament for rookie Superstars. The winner would get a special slot in the Royal Rumble.

If Mr. McMahon likes you, you'll become a rookie Superstar. You could enter the tournament and maybe even get into the Royal Rumble!

Of all the WWE events, the Royal Rumble is your favorite. It's a thirty-man brawl, and a new contestant enters the ring every ninety seconds. The only way to get eliminated is by going over the top rope. Last one standing is the winner.

You shake yourself out of your daydream. You've got an audition to get ready for!

The next afternoon, you show up at the gym for the tryout. Pete is there to greet you. He leads you to a locker room where a bunch of other guys are getting ready to audition, too. Some are bigger than you, and some are smaller than you. Everyone's in great shape. You suddenly realize that if you're going to impress Mr. McMahon, you're going to have to stand out from the crowd.

Pete calls your name, and you leave the locker room and step into the gym. There's an athlete waiting in the ring for you who looks to be the same height

and weight as you are. There's a bunch of guys in suits sitting in folding chairs around the ring, and one of them is Mr. McMahon. He looks just like he does on TV! Your heart starts to pump quickly.

"Okay," Pete says. "When the bell rings, I want you two guys to go at it. Show us your best moves."

You climb into the ring and shake hands with your opponent.

*Ding ding ding!*

The match begins, and you wrestle like you've never wrestled before. You break out your best aerial moves, dominating your opponent from the air. You even do a Shooting Star, jumping off the top rope and doing a backflip in midair.

After about five minutes, Pete stops the match. Mr. McMahon nods at your opponent.

"Sorry, kid. Keep training," he says in his gruff voice.

You take a deep breath. What will Mr. McMahon say about you?

"Nice moves," says the legendary WWE chairman. "You're a solid athlete. Now let's see if you can connect with an audience. Imagine you're talking to a camera and give me a monologue that tells me something about yourself."

You freeze. You've been so busy training your body

that you forgot another important part of being a WWE Superstar: personality.

"Um, uh, sure," you say nervously.

Your palms start to sweat. Your mind races as you try to think of something creative. You're generally a good guy in the ring. You could do a whole hero thing. But bad guys can get popular really quickly. Should you try to make the audience like you or hate you?

**If you deliver the monologue of a hero, go to page 21.**

**If you deliver the monologue of a villain, go to page 14.**

CONTINUED FROM PAGE 71

You start to sweat as the mammoth monster stomps down the aisle. Sure, you could be brave and attack him head on, but that would be foolish. If you want to win this Rumble, you've got to stay alive for the next ninety seconds.

Big Show is grinning as he climbs through the ropes. "Let's see how fresh you really are, rookie!"

He stomps after you. You dive to the mat and slide between his legs. The audience laughs. It's a cowardly move, but it'll keep you in the ring.

Big Show growls and turns around, swatting at you. You quickly do a backflip to avoid him.

It's the longest ninety seconds of your life. You flip and somersault all over the ring, avoiding Big Show. Finally, he manages to get hold of you. He dangles you in the air by your ankles.

"Enough is enough!" he says.

Just in time, Mark Henry's music begins to play. Big Show's head snaps toward the entrance, and he lets go of your ankle. You drop to the mat, but you're relieved. Big Show has set his sights on Mark Henry, the World's Strongest Man.

The two giants go at it, and you spend the next ninety seconds catching your breath. All those acrobatics have tired you out! Then the next Superstar enters the ring. It's Cody Rhodes, son of the "American Dream" Dusty Rhodes. He's a solid competitor who's just about your size.

You and Cody go at it, bouncing off the ropes to deliver punches and kicks to each other. Your adrenaline's really pumping, and you think you're starting to get the edge.

Before you know it, it's time for another Superstar to enter the ring. It's Evan Bourne! You're a huge fan of his high-flying skills in the ring. You've always wanted to face him, but you've almost got Cody eliminated.

**If you try to get Cody out of the ring, go to page 78.**

**If you go after Evan, go to page 88.**

CONTINUED FROM PAGE 63

You know there is no way you can ever take down a pro like John Cena at this point in your career. You could go out in a blaze of glory, but you feel like you've come too far to do that. There's still a chance you could win this thing, and you don't want to blow it.

You slide under the bottom rope. You can only stay out of the ring for thirty seconds or you'll be disqualified, so you have to be careful. But you're hoping that John Cena will find someone else to target while you're out.

That's exactly what happens. Cena goes after Santino Marella first, and it's not long before Marella goes flying out of the ring. At the same time, the Great Khali ousts his rival, Dolph Ziggler.

Now it's Cena versus Khali. Khali may be big, but Cena's combination of strength and skill are tough to beat. Cena gets Khali in a sleeperhold, weakening him. But before the giant can fall, Cena pounds him with a powerslam. The impact of the attack sends Khali falling backward over the top rope. You have to dodge to avoid getting hit by the giant. He slams into the ref as he hits the arena floor, and the ref is knocked out. That's good for you. It buys you more time outside the ring.

While all this is happening, three more Superstars have entered the ring. First, there's Matt Hardy. The young pro has won several championships and is known for his drive to win. Then there's Sheamus, the fiery Irish Superstar. Then fan favorite Kofi Kingston jumps into the ring, and the whole crowd shouts, "Here comes the boom!"

The audience is not so happy with you. They keep jeering at you to get back into the ring. But you know Cena is still in there, waiting for you.

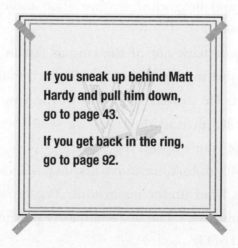

**If you sneak up behind Matt Hardy and pull him down, go to page 43.**

**If you get back in the ring, go to page 92.**

You know that hitting Morrison across the back with a chair isn't a legal move. It isn't a good guy move, either. But the urge to win this match overtakes you. You'll do anything to win!

You quickly grab a folding chair and slide into the ring. Then you stand up and whack Morrison across the back with the chair.

He cries out in pain and stumbles off The Miz. Furious, MVP storms into the ring. You hit him with the chair, and he goes down fast. The audience boos loudly at you.

You slide back out of the ring as fast as you can. The ref is just waking up. In the ring, The Miz is back on his feet. He pushes MVP out of the ring with his foot. Then he turns to Morrison, who's still bent over in agony from your hit with the chair.

The Miz grabs Morrison in a front face lock, tucking Morrison's head under his armpit. The crowd knows what's coming—it's The Miz's signature finishing move, the Mizard of Oz.

Morrison struggles to get out of the face lock, but

it's no use. The Miz falls backward, taking Morrison with him.

*Slam!* He twists Morrison around so the back of his head makes contact with the mat.

Now Morrison's out cold, but the ref is just fine. He counts the pinfall and declares you and The Miz the winners. You're the Unified WWE Tag Team Champions!

But now the crowd is booing you, and you realize you've ruined your whole good cop/bad cop thing. Now you're a bad guy, too!

Your popularity as a tag team drops, so you and The Miz break up and each of you goes solo again. You lose the Tag Team Championship title, too—after only one month.

It was amazing winning at the Royal Rumble, but it was bittersweet. You can't help wondering what might have happened if you hadn't picked up that folding chair.

## THE END

You decide to take a chance and deliver a bad guy monologue. The only problem is, you're not much of a bad guy. You search your brain for an idea. What makes you different than other Superstars? Then it hits you—you can use your young age and inexperience to your advantage.

You look into an imaginary camera like Mr. McMahon instructed you. Then you start riffing off the top of your head.

"Mr. McMahon, the reason you need me in WWE is because you need some young blood around here," you say. "When I tune in to watch *Raw,* I can't tell if I'm watching Superstars or an antiques show! Superstars these days are out of touch. Most of them think Facebook is the name of a new wrestling move!"

Mr. McMahon seems to like what you're doing, so you keep going. It's actually kind of fun.

"It's time to get the walkers and canes out of the ring, Mr. McMahon," you say in conclusion. "It's time for something fresh!"

Mr. McMahon is nodding his head. "That was great!" he says. "You've got the athletic skills and the personality to back it up. Pete was right. Congratulations. You're a WWE Superstar!"

"Woo-hoo!" You jump in the air and cheer. You've been working hard for this day for years, and now it's finally here.

"We'll call you Johnny Fresh," he says. "I'll have Pete work up the contracts. I want to get you on the road as soon as possible."

The sound of a cell phone ringing interrupts him, and Mr. McMahon reaches into his pocket to take the call. He nods.

"Mmmhmm. Mmmhmm," he says. "Don't worry. I've got it covered."

He flips his phone closed. "Kid, this is your lucky day. Evan Bourne was supposed to face Tyler Reks tonight on *SmackDown*, but he sprained his knee during training. How fast can you get on a plane?"

"As fast as you need me to!" you answer, your heart pounding. It's your first day as a Superstar, and you're going to be on *SmackDown*!

"Just give the crowd some more of what you gave me today," he says. "You'll be fine."

"I won't let you down," you promise.

The rest of the day is a whirlwind. You rush to the airport and get to the arena by late afternoon. Someone in the costume department suits you up in red shorts and black wrestling boots. Then you meet Tyler Reks before the match. You've always been a fan of this laid-back surfer dude. It's pretty cool to meet him in person.

"Nice to meet you," he says. "So, do you know what you're doing out there?"

"Mr. McMahon thinks I do," you say confidently.

Before you know it, the announcer calls you out into the ring.

"Presenting, for the first time on *SmackDown*, Johnny Fresh!"

The crowd doesn't know what to make of you. They've never seen you before, after all. When Tyler Reks comes out, they go crazy. You know you've got to make an impression—fast. So when Tyler starts to talk into the mic, you grab it from him.

"Easy now, old-timer!" you say. "Here, let me show you how to work this thing. I know you old folks have a hard time with this newfangled technology."

It's kind of ridiculous—Reks isn't old—but that's what makes your attitude funny. It's super obnoxious.

"I am not old!" Reks protests.

"Well, you're definitely not fresh!" you shoot back. "Not like me, Johnny Fresh. I'm as fresh as they come."

You pretend to sniff the air. "Ah, smell the freshness!"

You can tell you've rattled Tyler Reks. He lunges for you even before the bell rings. He reaches for your legs, and you figure he's going for one of his signature moves, a flapjack, where he'll toss you in the air like a pancake so you land flat on your back.

But today really is your lucky day. Reks loses his footing and slips. You quickly cover him, getting the pin. You win your first match!

You leave the ring with your arms in the air. Some fans are even cheering for you. It feels great!

Backstage, the other Superstars congratulate you. One of the other newcomers, a wrestler named IT, approaches you.

"Hey, Fresh, want to go to a party after the event tonight?" he asks. "I hear a lot of the big Superstars will be there. We'll get to meet guys we've been fans of our whole lives!"

If you go back to your hotel room and hit the sack, go to page 27.

If you go to the party, go to page 67.

You decide to go for the half nelson slam. You are able to pull off the move, which allows you to slam Masters back-first into the mat.

You've knocked the wind out of him. You nod to Tyson Kidd, and he helps you drag Masters to the rope and push him over the top.

Masters is out! You and Kidd continue your brawl. As you're trading blows with him, you see John Cena force Sheamus out of the ring. On the other side of the rope, Kofi Kingston flies off the top rope, knocking down Matt Hardy. Matt stumbles against the ropes, and Kofi lifts him up by the legs and flips him backward, eliminating him.

While all this is happening, more wrestlers enter the ring. Edge goes right for John Cena. William Regal, Christian, and Caylen Croft are also in the ring, and it's hard to see who's attacking who.

You clothesline Sheamus and he stumbles backward, bumping into Kofi Kingston. Kingston quickly lifts him up and sends him flying out of the ring.

You quickly assess the situation. Your best bet is

to take on a guy who you might be able to beat. You know you're not experienced enough to fight Kofi or Christian. That leaves Caylen Croft, who's about your size, and William Regal, a snobby Brit.

**If you go after William Regal, go to page 31.**

**If you go after Caylen Croft, go to page 56.**

You decide to stay true to yourself. You take a deep breath and pretend to look at an imaginary camera like Mr. McMahon instructed you to.

"Ever since I was a kid, I've dreamed of becoming a WWE Superstar," you begin. You deliver a heartfelt monologue about how hard you've trained to achieve your dream.

When you're done, Mr. McMahon doesn't say anything for a minute. Your heart sinks. Did you blow it?

"Not bad, but not great, either," Mr. McMahon says. "You need to work on your mic skills. But you're an impressive athlete. Tell you what—I'll give you a chance."

You can't believe it! "Thank you so much," you say. "I won't let you down."

"Maybe, maybe not," Mr. McMahon says. "Just to make sure, I'm putting you on probation. I'll make you a Superstar, but you've got one month to prove you have what it takes. If you don't improve your game by then, you're out."

"I plan to stick around," you say confidently.

You climb out of the ring, your heart pounding with excitement. You're a WWE Superstar!

Pete sees the grin on your face. "Congratulations, kid," he says. "You're lucky Mr. McMahon is giving you a chance."

He glances down at a clipboard. "I can put you in a match on Tuesday in Ohio." He hands you a pile of papers. "I need you to report to the arena on noon that day. Fill these out and bring them with you. I'll see you in a few days."

You rush home and pack a bag for your trip. You have enough money for a bus ticket to Ohio. It's a long time to be on the road, and you spend hours watching WWE videos on your phone. You pay attention to the speeches the Superstars give in the ring, trying to pick up some tips.

Your bus arrives in Ohio on Tuesday morning, and you take a cab to the arena. It's bigger than any other venue you've performed in before. You still can't believe it—tonight you'll be performing in front of thousands of people!

Pete spots you and takes you to the costume room where you're assigned a pair of blue shorts and brand-new wrestling boots. Then he leads you to the locker room.

"You're going to be wrestling Drew McIntyre tonight," he tells you, and you stop in your tracks.

Drew's a wrestler from Scotland who's ruthless in the ring. He's also 6'5", which is half a foot taller than you are.

Pete sees the worried look on your face. "Hey, you've got to start somewhere, kid."

When you get to the locker room, you find Drew brushing his long hair in the mirror. You walk up to him, trying to look confident.

"Hi," you say, introducing yourself. "Looks like we'll be facing each other tonight."

Drew turns to face you. "Oh, really?" he asks.

"Yeah," you say. "Mr. McMahon signed me himself."

"Oh, he did, did he?" Drew asks, and he doesn't sound very friendly. "I'm looking forward to it."

Then he walks away.

As it gets closer to the show, you start to get more excited. WWE Superstars fill the locker room. Chris Jericho. Big Show. Yoshi Tatsu. You feel like you're in a dream!

Your match with Drew is the first of the night. The announcer calls your name first. You walk to the ring. There are so many people in the stands! A few people clap for you, but not many. They don't know you yet.

When Drew enters the arena, the crowd goes crazy. He jumps into the ring and grabs the mic from the announcer.

"My opponent here told me in the locker room that he's been chosen by Mr. McMahon," Drew says. "But everyone knows that *I* am the only Superstar officially endorsed by the chairman. This little punk is a liar!"

"Um, that's not really what I meant—," you say, but the bell rings. Before you can make a move, Drew gets you with an elbow to the chest.

You never recover. Drew spends the next three minutes punishing you. He grabs your head under his elbow and slams you on the mat with a suplex. Then he picks you up and finishes with a Double Underhook DDT, dropping you to the mat face-first. You don't know what hit you.

"Loser! Loser! Loser!" the crowd chants.

You pick yourself up and exit the ring, humiliated. Backstage, you see Chris Jericho waiting in the wings.

"Don't feel bad, kid," he tells you. "You're new. I got pounded my first time in the ring, too."

"Really?" you ask, feeling a little better.

"Sure," Chris says. "But you know what might help? Develop a personality that the audience can latch on to. Think about it: Undertaker. Mankind. Some of the biggest Superstars have cool identities."

"It's hard to think of one," you say.

"I've got one for you," Chris says. "Kid Caveman! You can carry a big club and everything. It's great. I wish I had thought of it years ago."

You're not sure what to say. Kid Caveman sounds kind of lame. But Chris Jericho is one of the biggest Superstars around. Maybe you should take his advice.

**If you become Kid Caveman, go to page 40.**

**If you decide to keep your own name, go to page 58.**

You've just gotten into the ring, and you're too excited to leave now. Confident, you begin to climb the ropes. Then you feel two strong hands grip you around the chest.

You try to hold on to the ropes, but Mark Henry is too strong. He puts one hand around your neck and another around your abdomen, lifting you up. You know what's coming—the world's strongest slam. It's not going to be fun.

*Bam!* You collide with the mat, and the fall knocks the wind out of you. Henry rolls over and pins you, and the ref quickly counts you out.

Mark Henry and MVP win the match and will continue to the next match in the tournament. As you walk back to your corner, The Miz is shaking his head in disappointment.

"You should have tagged me!"

## THE END

It's tempting to go and hang out with your favorite WWE Superstars, but you know if you play your cards right you'll spend plenty of time with them during your long career in WWE.

"That sounds awesome, but I'd better not," you say. "I've had a really long day, and I have to report for training tomorrow."

Early the next morning, you show up at a local gym for some more training. You meet your coach, Barry, a strong guy who's built like a bulldog. Barry works with you for hours, teaching you some new moves and helping you finesse the moves you already know.

"You need to pump up your aerial moves," Barry tells you. "They need to be stronger if you want to take your opponent down to the mat."

You take a break for lunch, and, while you're eating, Pete walks in with a big smile on his face.

"You were great last night," he says. "And Barry likes you, too. Mr. McMahon's really happy. He wants me to tell you that you can compete for the newcomer slot in the Royal Rumble."

"Woo-hoo!" You jump out of your seat and start dancing around.

"The tournament begins next week," Pete tells you. "You can work with Barry until then. Good luck!"

You fly to Connecticut for the week and train with Barry at the WWE headquarters.

"Let's work on your frog splash," he suggests.

That's the move you used the night Pete saw you compete. First, you make sure that your opponent is lying flat on his back with his head and feet pointing to the corners of the ring. Then you climb the opposite corner and leap off, extending your arms and legs like a frog at the last minute to cover your opponent's stomach. It puts you in prime position to pin him and end the match.

Barry recruits another wrestler, the newcomer IT, to help you train. You demonstrate your frog splash for Barry. IT groans as you make contact.

"Not bad," Barry says. "But you're supposed to be the fresh kid, right? You should put your own twist on it."

That sounds good to you. With Barry's help, you try a variation of a corkscrew frog splash where you make a one-hundred-and-eighty-degree turn in midair. It adds some extra power—plus, it looks really cool.

Finally, the night of your first tournament match arrives. You'll be on *SmackDown* again, wrestling Zack Ryder. The Long Island Loudmouth is known for his purple headband, cocky attitude, and signature cry of "woo woo woo . . . you know it!"

When the match begins, Ryder starts out strong. After pummeling you with some strategic kicks, he wraps his elbow around your head and drops to the ground so you hit your head against his shoulder. You're dizzy, but you're able to get up before he can pin you. You counter with a clothesline that sends Ryder sprawling on the mat.

You're losing, and you need a big comeback. Should you try your new corkscrew frog splash?

**If you try the frog splash, go to page 55.**

**If you stick to your ground game, go to page 69.**

The Great Khali is more than seven feet tall and four hundred twenty pounds. You and The Miz might be able to take him if you work together.

You nod back to The Miz.

"Let's climb," he tells you. "We can launch an aerial attack and take him down from above."

It sounds like a good idea to you. You and The Miz climb the top rope. The Great Khali just sneers at you both. He reminds you of King Kong, snatching planes from the air on top of the Empire State Building. He'll probably do the same to you.

You think about climbing down, but you're too late. You feel a push from the side and turn to see The Miz's grinning face. He's taking you out!

"It's every man for himself," The Miz says.

"That's right," you say. You may be going down, but you won't be doing it alone. You grab The Miz's ankle on your way down and pull him to the floor with you.

"What were they thinking?" Jerry Lawler wonders.

**THE END**

**CONTINUED FROM PAGE 20**

You think that Regal's snobby ways and British accent might mean that he's not so tough in the ring—but you're dead wrong. Regal is experienced, skilled, and fresh to the ring, so he's full of energy.

He's also the master of the suplex, a punishing move that a wrestler uses to drive his opponent into the mat using the force of his own weight. Regal decides to suplex you until you can't fight back.

And that's exactly what he does. *Bam! Bam! Bam!* He slams you into the mat over and over again until you're exhausted. You don't even realize it when he's tossing you over the rope. The next thing you know, you're on the arena floor looking up at the ring.

"And Johnny Fresh is out!" Jerry Lawler cries.

You groan. Maybe attacking William Regal wasn't such a great idea.

## THE END

CONTINUED FROM PAGE 60

You know that winning the Royal Rumble is a long shot. But if you team with The Miz, there's a much better chance that you'll win the Unified WWE Tag Team Championship at the event. He's already won the WWE Tag Team Championship, the World Tag Team Championship, and the Unified Tag Team Championship. And he's been the United States Champion. It's amazing that he wants to partner with a rookie like you.

"I'll do it," you say. "But I'm confused. I mean, I'm a good guy in the ring, and you're, well . . ."

"I can't help it if people don't like The Miz!" he shoots back. "They're just jealous. But I think we can make it work. We could do a good cop/bad cop thing. I'll wear black and you can wear white."

"Like yin and yang," you say. "That's pretty cool."

"Of course it's cool!" The Miz snaps. "All of my ideas are cool. How do you think I got to be such a big Superstar?"

The Miz is conceited, but you don't care. He has a lot more experience than you do, and you want to learn.

First, you plan your strategy. The Miz wants revenge on his old tag team partner, John Morrison. Morrison and his new partner, R-Truth, hold the championship, and The Miz wants it back. Morrison and R-Truth have issued a challenge: They're holding a tournament for all interested tag teams. The winner will face them at the Royal Rumble, and they'll put the championship on the line.

There are eight tag teams who want to compete, including you and The Miz. That means you'll have to win three matches before you can face Morrison and R-Truth.

Your first match will be against MVP and Mark Henry.

In the days leading up to the match, you and The Miz practice together as much as you can. The Miz uses a mix of power moves, like a discus punch, as well as some aerial moves. During a tag team match there will be a few times when you'll be able to wrestle at the same time. You work out some double-team moves.

Before you know it, it's time for your match with MVP and Mark Henry. The Miz and Mark Henry start out in the ring first. You hang back outside your corner. If The Miz needs you, he'll tag you.

Your heart races as you watch The Miz and Mark Henry go at it. The Miz charges at him. Mark Henry

grabs him and tosses him toward the ropes. The Miz goes flying over the side.

You can't believe it. You're in! You climb on top of the rope and dive into the ring, hoping to knock down the World's Strongest Man. But he quickly moves out of the way.

The Miz is back on his feet. "Tag me!" he yells from the corner of the ring.

**If you tag The Miz, go to page 74.**

**If you don't tag The Miz, go to page 26.**

CONTINUED FROM PAGE 63

You know you're no match for John Cena. If he's got his sights set on you, you're done. So you may as well go out with a bang.

You climb the ropes, figuring you can dive onto Cena and knock him down on the mat. Maybe by then someone else will come into the ring who can help you out. You stand on the rope, arms outstretched, and work the crowd.

"Can you feel the freshness?" you ask, and your fans cheer wildly.

Then you dive . . . and Cena assaults you in midair, knocking you down! Then he picks you up and carries you on his back, fireman style. Instead of slamming you into the mat, he walks over to the ropes and dumps you out of the ring.

"I gotta say one thing about Johnny Fresh," Jerry Lawler says. "That kid has guts!"

You're bruised, battered, and beaten, but you still feel great. You stand up and wave to your cheering fans as you leave the arena.

**THE END**

You're feeling confident in your frog splash. First, though, you've got to knock down R-Truth. He tries to get you in a face lock, but you avoid him by stomping on his foot with all your might. As he hops up and down in pain, you bounce off the rope to add some momentum to your next attack.

*Wham!* You get him with a clothesline. He stumbles and falls backward.

You don't have much time. As quickly as you can, you climb the corner rope. You leap, corkscrewing in midair and then extending your arms and legs.

The crowd goes wild. You slam into R-Truth, and his body shakes from the impact. He's weak. But you still have to get him over the top rope.

It's not easy. You lift him up and push him over the top rope with all of your might.

To your amazement, he goes over. You've ousted R-Truth!

"Johnny Fresh is really proving himself in the ring tonight," Michael Cole says from the announcers' booth.

You're feeling really proud. When you turn back to the ring, you see that a lot's been going on while you were busy with R-Truth. The Great Khali has entered the ring, along with Kane and The Miz. Kane's in the wrong place at the wrong time, and the Great Khali easily ousts him. Then he takes out both Mark Henry and Big Show, who are exhausted from their nonstop battle.

Now it's you, The Miz, and the Great Khali. The Miz nods at you, and you realize he wants to team up.

If you take your chances alone, go to page 62.

If you agree to team up with The Miz, go to page 30.

Ezekiel Jackson and Drew McIntyre are both tough opponents. Jackson held the last ECW Championship title in history. McIntyre is taller, but Jackson is built like a truck and has a tough reputation.

You figure you're going to get creamed either way, so you go after Jackson. He stops you in your tracks, gripping you in a bear hug. You struggle to get out, but you're running out of energy fast.

You kick your way out and slide under the top rope to get another thirty seconds of rest. Jackson climbs up the ropes and starts yelling at you to come back in. Drew McIntyre sees this and pushes Jackson over the top!

Angry at being eliminated, Jackson starts chasing you around the ring. You have no choice but to get back inside. The ref starts yelling at him to leave the ring area.

While the ref's distracted, Edge returns! He's angry at Christian for eliminating him earlier. He slides into the ring unnoticed while Christian is eliminating Drew McIntyre. Then he attacks Christian from behind, lifting him up and throwing him out of the ring. He slips away before the ref can see him.

You, for one, don't plan on telling the ref what happened. You're happy to have Christian out of the way. Now you're in the ring with Kofi Kingston, who's battling Rey Mysterio. Jack Swagger has entered and is trying to attack Kofi.

Then Chris Jericho's theme music blares through the arena.

"He's number thirty! Chris Jericho is number thirty!" Jerry Lawler announces.

You can't believe your luck. The Royal Rumble is coming to an end, and you're still a contender! Is it possible that you could actually win this thing?

Go to page 81.

You decide to take Chris Jericho's advice. You're on probation, after all, and you've got to do something to make the audience like you. Jericho has been in the business a long time. He might be onto something.

That night, you talk to the people in the costume department about your idea. Your next match in Tennessee is two days away. By the time you get to the arena, they have a new costume waiting for you.

You trade in your red shorts for a tiger-striped loincloth and a big club that looks like a dinosaur bone. You check yourself out in the mirror—and you look really silly.

"Are you sure this is going to work?" you ask the woman who's given you the costume.

She shrugs. "You wanted caveman, I gave you caveman. It's up to you to make it work."

Chris Jericho sees you in the hallway and slaps you on the back.

"Great job, kid!" he says. "Perfect! You're going to wow them!"

You hope he's right. You're wrestling Drew again,

and this time you want to win. When you get to the ring, you grab the mic.

"Hello, Tennessee! I am Kid Caveman!" you yell.

Some people clap, and others boo. Most aren't sure what to make of you.

Drew enters the ring, takes one look at you, and starts laughing.

"Are you serious?" he asks. When the bell rings, he takes your club from you and smashes it over your head. The match only lasts about two minutes this time. As you leave, you hear the crowd's chant:

"Loser! Loser! Loser!"

Backstage, you find Chris Jericho actually rolling on the floor, laughing.

"I can't believe you fell for it!" he says. "Kid Caveman! No hard feelings, okay, kid? It's tradition to welcome the rookies with a prank."

Tradition or not, you're steamed. You feel like bodyslamming Jericho for what he's done.

If you jump Jericho,
go to page 51.

If you decide to prove
him wrong by making
Kid Caveman a popular
character, go to page 72.

CONTINUED FROM PAGE 11

Matt Hardy knocks down Kofi Kingston and then climbs to the top rope to try to finish him off. You climb up on the apron of the ring and grab Matt by his shorts, pulling him down. A surprised Matt hits the floor. He turns to you, furious.

You scramble back into the ring, and Matt follows you.

"Hey, you can't do that!" you protest. "I eliminated you!"

"The ref doesn't know that," Matt replies, pointing down at the still groggy referee.

That's when you realize you're in big trouble. Matt grips you in a reverse face lock, tightly wrapping his elbow around your neck as you face away from him. Then he falls to the ground, slamming your face into the mat.

You're as limp as a piece of spaghetti. Matt pulls you up and pitches you out of the ring. You won't win the Royal Rumble, but at least you got pretty far.

**THE END**

CONTINUED FROM PAGE 76

It might be illegal, but you can't just stand there and let your partner get pounded. You jump in the ring and pull Luke Gallows off The Miz, slamming him onto the mat. He stands up and glares at you, furious. You bounce off the rope with your right arm extended and whack him across the chest.

The clothesline works! Gallows slams backward onto the mat. The Miz has broken out of the chokehold that CM Punk had on him and is pummeling him with punches once more.

Gallows gets to his feet and charges at you. Behind him, you see the ref slowly lifting his head. You quickly run back to your corner and duck under the ropes.

"Gallows! Back in your corner!" the ref barks.

The Miz bodyslams a weakened Punk, sending him to the mat. Then he drops down and makes the pin. You can't believe it. You've won the second match!

"Thanks for your help out there," The Miz tells you, and it feels good knowing you did the right thing.

That same night, the remaining two tag teams face off to see who will face you in the finals. You hear the results backstage: It's the Hart Dynasty.

"No way," you say.

David Hart Smith, Tyson Kidd, and Natalya are all connected to the legendary family of Canadian wrestlers, the Hart family. Some of the best Superstars in the world were trained in Stu Hart's "dungeon," including Hall of Famer Bret Hart. Smith is a beast at two hundred sixty pounds, and Kidd is a master of execution. They're not going to be easy to beat.

Smith, Kidd, and Natalya run backstage, cheering as their theme music is played. They stop when they see you and The Miz.

"Why don't you two just throw in the towel right now?" Smith asks. "You don't stand a chance of beating us."

"We'll fry you up like Canadian bacon," The Miz counters.

"Ha!" Kidd laughs. "A self-absorbed poser and a kid right out of kindergarten? What planet are you living on?"

You realize that remark about the kindergarten kid was aimed at you, and you start to get angry. The Miz is already fuming.

"You think we're satisfied to coast on the reputations of our daddies?" he asks. "We got where

we are by hard work and training."

Natalya nods at you. "More like potty training," she says with a sneer.

"Nobody talks to my partner like that!" The Miz yells. "You want to make this more interesting? I say we make this next match a TLC Match!"

You can't believe what you've just heard. In WWE, "TLC" stands for "Tables, Ladders & Chairs." A TLC Match is an anything goes, all-out brawl. You've seen Superstars get really hurt during those matches.

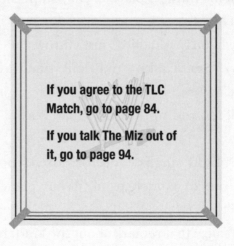

If you agree to the TLC Match, go to page 84.

If you talk The Miz out of it, go to page 94.

You start to sweat as the mammoth monster stomps down the aisle toward you. Normally, Big Show's got a deadly serious look on his face, but right now he's smiling. You can tell he's looking forward to making an example of you in front of this huge crowd.

You have a choice: You could run around the ring like a chicken for ninety seconds and maybe survive, or you can be brave and foolish and attack him head on.

You go for brave and foolish. As soon as Big Show steps into the ring, you charge at him.

"*Aaaaaaaaaaaaaaaaaaaah!*"

Big Show doesn't even budge. He grabs you by the wrist, grinning. Then he tosses you over the rope like a rag doll.

You're out! The crowd cheers.

Jerry Lawler and Michael Cole are commentating on the match. As you slink back down the aisle, you hear Lawler say, "I think that was the fastest anyone's ever been ejected from the Rumble!"

You smile. You may be out of the Rumble, but at least you're a record breaker!

## THE END

Something in your gut tells you that a bodyslam is the way to go. The crowd starts to stomp their feet as they see you get ready to make your move. You feel the rhythm course through your body, and it gives you strength.

You feel stronger than you ever have before.

*"Aaaaaaaaaaaaaaaah!"*

With a loud battle cry, you charge across the ring, grab Kofi around the chest, and slam him into the mat. He's dazed. You pick him up again, and this time you push him into the ropes.

You've got so much force behind you that Kofi backflips right over the top rope. He reaches out to stop himself from falling, but he's moving too fast. Then he hits the floor.

There's a stunned silence for a second. Then the arena erupts in thunderous applause.

"He's done it! Johnny Fresh has done it! Johnny Fresh has won the Royal Rumble!" Jerry Lawler shouts.

Confetti falls from the ceiling. The reporters covering the event start snapping photos of you,

blinding you with bright flashes of white light. You raise your arms in victory and let the confetti fall on your arms and face.

You've done it all. You were nobody until the day you impressed Mr. McMahon with your audition. You beat other newcomers for a slot in the Royal Rumble. You drew the number one slot—the most unlucky slot in the whole Rumble. You faced Kofi Kingston one-on-one to win the Rumble.

You have no idea where your career in WWE will lead, but right now you wouldn't care if it all ended tomorrow. After all, how could it get any better than this?

## THE END

"That wasn't funny!" you yell, blinded with rage. You throw your body on top of Chris Jericho's and pull your arm back to throw a punch. But Chris stops you with one strong hand.

"Settle down there, Caveman," he says, tossing you aside.

You slide across the tile floor. A crowd of Superstars has gathered backstage to watch what's happening. You know what you're doing isn't smart, but you can't help yourself. You charge at Jericho, who's now on his feet, planning to deliver a head butt to his chest. This time, he picks you up and flips you over. Then he pulls your arms behind your back.

"Chill out, rookie," he says. "If you're going to be a WWE Superstar, you're going to have to learn some self-control."

You realize he's right, and you're suddenly embarrassed. Attacking Jericho was a stupid idea. Your face flushes as you walk through the crowd of onlookers back to the locker room.

You change out of your Kid Caveman costume.

Pete walks into the locker room.

"I'll never wear that again," you say, sheepishly holding up the loincloth.

"That's for sure," Pete tells you. "Fighting in the locker room area is prohibited in your contract. Sorry, kid. Mr. McMahon heard about it and sent word from HQ. You're fired."

You shake your head in disbelief. You had one chance to become a WWE Superstar—and you blew it!

## THE END

CONTINUED FROM PAGE 76

It's a tough decision, but you decide to stay in your corner. That's what The Miz wants, right?

Unfortunately, The Miz can't tell you what he wants because CM Punk has him in a headlock while Luke Gallows stomps on his foot. It's painful to watch. Then Gallows picks up The Miz by his feet, and he and Punk swing your partner back and forth.

*Bam!* They slam him down on the mat.

At that moment, the ref starts to wake up. Gallows quickly gets back to his corner. When the ref gets back on his feet, he sees Punk pinning The Miz to the mat.

The crowd starts to boo.

"It's not fair!" you yell. "Gallows was in the ring illegally."

But the ref only knows what he sees. He starts the count.

"One . . . two . . . three!"

CM Punk starts pumping his fists in the air. You jump into the ring and run to The Miz's side.

Your partner is getting up slowly.

"What happened?" he asks.

"Punk and Gallows teamed up on you," you tell him. "The ref came to and counted you out."

"No!" The Miz shouts angrily. He jumps to his feet. "Why didn't you come in and help me?"

"You told me not to be a hero," you explain.

"But you've got to know when to come in and when to stay back," he says, shaking his head. "You're too green. I should have known."

"I'll learn," you promise. "Next time, I'll—"

"There won't be a next time!" The Miz snaps. "You're not my partner anymore!"

## THE END

Even though you're dizzy, you decide you need to try your corkscrew frog splash. You really need to get the crowd on your side, and this move will surely do it.

The crowd cheers as you climb the ropes. You dive off the top rope, turning your body in midair.

But the key to doing the move is to turn at exactly the right time. You start your turn too late, and instead of landing on Zack Ryder, you land to the side—and your feet hit first. A sharp pain shoots through your ankle.

Ryder rolls over on you and pins you. He's won the match! You've lost your chance to compete in the Royal Rumble.

But that's not all. You've broken your ankle, so you won't be able to wrestle for a few months. You're on the sidelines—just as you were getting hot.

## THE END

CONTINUED FROM PAGE 20

Caylen Croft is closer to you in size and experience, so you decide to challenge him. He's got his back to you, so you run and jump on his back, hoping to toss him against the ropes. But Caylen easily tosses you off.

You can tell he's eager to brawl, and you start to wonder if you made the right choice. He runs toward you and then wraps his elbow around your neck, slamming you down onto the mat.

Before you can get up from the neckbreaker, Caylen climbs onto the second rope, springboards off, and lands with his leg extended over your chest. You know he's angling for the pin, but something deep inside you kicks in. You shove Caylen off you, and he goes stumbling backward.

It's lucky that Caylen lands in the path of Kofi Kingston, who's in the middle of launching a kick at his opponent. The kick lands on the back of Caylen's head, and he goes down. You quickly climb the rope. It's time for your corkscrew frog splash again.

Once again, you execute the move perfectly, slamming into Caylen. His body is limp, so you lift him up and pitch him over the ropes.

"And Johnny Fresh has just eliminated another Superstar!" Michael Cole announces.

You turn back to the ring and realize that John Cena and Edge have eliminated each other! William Regal is out, too. Kofi Kingston is still in, and he's battling masked Superstar Rey Mysterio. Christian is still in, too, and he's going at it with Yoshi Tatsu. Drew McIntyre and Ezekiel Jackson are also in the ring.

If you go after Drew McIntyre, go to page 86.

If you go after Ezekiel Jackson, go to page 38.

"I think I'll stick to being myself," you tell Chris Jericho. "But thanks."

He shrugs. "I'm telling you, you could be famous."

As you head back to the locker room, Kofi Kingston walks up to you. He's such a huge Superstar—and he starts talking to you!

"I overheard what Jericho was telling you," he says. "Good thing you didn't listen to him. He likes to play tricks on all the new guys."

"Thanks," you say, and you're feeling more confident knowing that you've made the right choice.

You travel to the next arena and face Drew McIntyre again. This time, you're sure to talk into the mic first.

"Drew McIntyre's going to come up here and tell you he's the Chosen One," you say. "And that's fine. I don't need to hide in Mr. McMahon's shadow to win!"

He beats you again, but you get in some good shots. This time, the crowd doesn't chant "loser."

Your next match is against Jack Swagger. He's just as tall as McIntyre and weighs two hundred sixty pounds. At first you're sure he's going to wipe the mat with you, but you stay confident. You stick to your high-flying moves and, to your surprise, you pin him!

A writer on a fansite dubs you the "Giant Killer." You're starting to gain some popularity. After a month is over, Mr. McMahon sends you a message:

*Congratulations! I'm extending your contract. I still haven't decided if you'll compete for the newcomer slot in the Royal Rumble. Keep doing what you're doing and we'll see.*

You let out a cheer. You're one step closer to your dream! But there's another surprise for you that day.

The Miz approaches you before a match in Oklahoma. The popular Superstar has a reputation as a bad guy. You've never met him before. But he knows all about you.

"I want you to become my tag team partner," The Miz tells you. "I want my Tag Team Championship back. John Morrison and R-Truth have the championship now, and they don't deserve it. I want to take it from them at a special match at the Royal Rumble."

You're shocked. Teaming with The Miz would be huge! So would competing in a tag team match at the Royal Rumble.

There's only one problem. If you team with The Miz, you won't be able to compete for the newcomer slot. You'd lose your chance to compete in the thirty-man match—and be the first rookie to win the Royal Rumble.

"So what'll it be?" The Miz asks.

If you tag team with The Miz, go to page 32.

If you decline The Miz's offer, go to page 68.

You're not sure if you should try your corkscrew frog splash yet. You spin and aim a kick at his chest, but R-Truth grabs your leg with one arm. Then he reaches behind your back with his other arm. You brace yourself for what's coming.

*Wham!* R-Truth powerslams you into the mat. You don't know what hit you. Your whole body hurts.

R-Truth picks you up and tries to push you over the top rope. You grab on, trying to stay in the ring, but he's stronger than you. With one mighty push, he hurls you out of the ring.

You're out of the Rumble!

"I should have tried the corkscrew frog splash," you mutter as you begin the walk of shame back to the locker room.

## THE END

CONTINUED FROM PAGE 37

You shake your head no. The Royal Rumble is every man for himself, and you can't be sure that The Miz isn't holding a grudge against you for refusing to become his tag team partner.

The Miz just shrugs. The Great Khali stomps toward both of you. At more than seven feet tall and four hundred twenty pounds, he's just as intimidating as Big Show.

Your acrobatics worked when you were in the ring with Big Show before, so you try the same tactic. You flip around the ring, avoiding the Great Khali. He treats you like an annoying fly and turns his attention to The Miz.

Before the ninety seconds are over, the Great Khali has thrown The Miz over the top rope. He turns his attention back to you, but at that moment the next Superstar enters the ring: Dolph Ziggler. He and Khali are old rivals, so Khali forgets all about you.

Santino Marella enters the ring next. Santino likes to pound, punch, and punish his opponents. You've been in the ring for a while now, and you're starting to feel it. But Santino is fresh. He starts to wail on you, hitting you with a barrage of punches.

You do your best to fight back and manage to keep him at bay. Then the crowd starts to go crazy. You and Santino stop to see who's coming in the ring next. It's John Cena!

To your surprise, the Superstar points right at you. "Fresh, your time is up!" he cries.

**If you climb the ropes for an aerial attack, go to page 35.**

**If you slip through the bottom rope to avoid Cena, go to page 10.**

CONTINUED FROM PAGE 96

"Ladies and gentlemen, it's finally time for the Royal Rumble!"

The announcer's voice echoes through the arena as the Royal Rumble begins. You've wrestled on TV since you became a Superstar, but there's something about a big event like this that just feels different. The air is alive with excitement. Even backstage the other Superstars seem to be more pumped up and energized than you've ever seen them.

It's contagious. You feel like you're going to jump out of your white boots. Luckily, the Unified WWE Tag Team Championship is the first match of the night. Then you'll be able to kick back and watch the thirty-man main event from backstage. But will you be doing it as a newcomer—or as a champion?

You hear the announcer call your names, and the music swells. You and The Miz walk down the aisle to the ring, and the crowd goes crazy. You're more popular than ever since you beat the Hart Dynasty. People seem to like you and The Miz as a team.

When Morrison and R-Truth come out, you see

The Miz's face turn to stone. He's got a lot of history with both of them. You remember the first time The Miz approached you to ask you to be his partner. This is what it's all about: revenge.

After the announcer spells out the terms of the match, the bell rings. The Miz starts out first, as usual, and he's facing Morrison.

Morrison is on fire, going after The Miz with a series of roundhouse kicks. The Miz jumps over them, finally taking charge and grabbing Morrison's left leg in midair, twisting it behind his back. In pain, Morrison reaches out and tags MVP.

To your surprise, The Miz tags you in!

"Your turn," he says with a grin. "Let's see what you can do."

This is the first time The Miz has ever trusted you like this, and you don't want to let him down. You size up MVP. He's not as physically huge as some of the Superstars you've faced, but you know he's a fan of power moves. If you let him get control, you'll be in trouble.

You decide to take to the ropes. It's risky, but it's what you do best. You springboard from one side of the ring to the other, bouncing off the ropes. MVP looks frustrated. You're moving fast, and he can't catch you.

Then you jump up and aim a thrust kick at his chest.

The move doesn't work. MVP grabs your leg, stopping you, and then throws you into the ropes. You tumble over the side, knocking into the ref.

The ref is out cold. You get to your feet and see that Morrison is back in the ring with The Miz. Morrison spins and delivers a powerful kick to The Miz's chest.

*Bam!* The Miz goes down. Morrison plants a foot on his chest. You start to panic. You've got to help The Miz somehow. It can't end like this!

**If you grab a chair and hit Morrison, go to page 12.**

**If you wait and see what The Miz can do, go to page 90.**

CONTINUED FROM PAGE 18

Going to a party on your first night as a WWE Superstar? Not smart, but it's sure to be lots of fun!

You've had a long day and you're exhausted. You have a great time at the party, and you meet some of your favorite Superstars—but you stay up way too late. In the morning, you sleep right through your alarm clock and report to the gym for training two hours late.

Mr. McMahon is not pleased. That's not the kind of behavior he wants from one of his Superstars. He delivers the news to you through Pete.

"You're on probation," Pete tells you. "You won't be going on TV anytime soon."

"What about the newcomer tournament for the slot in the Royal Rumble?" you ask.

"No way!" Pete says. "You really blew it, kid."

## THE END

"Thanks," you tell The Miz. "But my solo career is going pretty well right now. I'm trying to win a spot in the thirty-man match at the Royal Rumble."

The Miz shakes his head. "You're missing out on the chance of a lifetime. What rookie wouldn't want to team up with a huge Superstar like The Miz?"

The Miz has a point, but you've made your choice, and there's no turning back. You've got to impress Mr. McMahon so he'll give you a slot in the newcomer tournament.

But your "Giant Killer" nickname starts to work against you. Some of the more experienced Superstars don't like being shown up by a skinny rookie. They're relentless in the ring, and you start losing matches again—and even worse, you're losing popularity.

When Mr. McMahon announces the names of the newcomers who will compete, you're not on the list.

"Sorry, kid," he tells you. "Maybe next year."

## THE END

Something tells you that doing your corkscrew frog splash wouldn't be a good idea right now. You need to focus on winning the match, not winning over the crowd.

Ryder's down, so you take advantage of that. You sit down and twist his legs like a pretzel. Ryder struggles to get away, but he can't do it. He taps out, and you hear the bell ring.

You've won your first match of the tournament! You're super confident. You cut down the rest of the newcomers in the tournament like a jungle explorer with a machete.

You're going to the Royal Rumble!

In the days leading up to the event, you train like you've never trained before. Finally, the night of the Royal Rumble arrives.

The air in the arena is filled with energy. You've been on TV with WWE several times now, but this feels different. It's a big night. Championships are on the line. And one Superstar will surpass twenty-nine opponents to win the ultimate challenge: the Royal Rumble.

It's chaotic in the locker room. As always, Mr. McMahon keeps the list of Superstars who will be competing a secret. The order of when Superstars enter the ring is a secret, too. The number you get can play a big part in whether you win or lose. If you're number thirty, you may only have to defeat a few guys to win it all. But if you're number one, you've got to face every other opponent in the ring.

You look around, trying to figure out who will be in the Rumble with you. For the first time, you start to feel nervous. There are some real legends around you. You're still just a rookie, after all. What will happen if you have to go one-on-one with one of them in the ring?

The thirty-man bout is the final match of the night. You watch the championship matches from the locker room, getting more nervous each minute. Finally, it's time for the Rumble to begin.

Unlike other matches, the announcer won't be calling out names. Pete shows up with a clipboard that contains the roster on it. When he taps you, you're in.

"It's time for the ROYAL RUMBLE!" the announcer cheers into the mic. The crowd goes wild. Pete taps you on the shoulder.

"All right, kid. You're in!"

You freeze for a minute. You've got the number

one slot! Behind you, the other wrestlers start to laugh.

You take a deep breath.

"I got this," you say.

Then you step out into the arena. After your performance in the tournament, you've become a crowd favorite. They cheer wildly as you walk out into the ring.

You stand in the ring, eyeing the arena entrance. A wrestler is going to walk out of there. And whoever it is, you'll be stuck one-on-one for ninety seconds until the next wrestler is tapped.

Familiar theme music starts to play. Your heart sinks as a wrestler steps into the arena.

It's Big Show!

If you attack Big Show, go to page 47.

If you try to avoid him, go to page 8.

You need to cool down—and quickly. Attacking Chris Jericho backstage would end your career before it even started.

"Ha. Very funny, Jericho," you say. "But guess what? I'm going to keep up this Kid Caveman thing. I'll make it popular."

Chris shakes his head. "Man, if you can do that, I'll be impressed."

You're not sure why you made that promise—but you don't want Chris Jericho to get the best of you. You spend all your free time coming up with funny lines for your monologue.

"I took down a woolly mammoth for dinner yesterday. And he was a lot bigger—and hairier—than you!"

"Beating you is so easy, a caveman could do it!"

It's a little bit corny, but the crowd seems to like it. For the rest of the month you wrestle night after night in state after state, and the crowd stops chanting "loser" and is now chanting "Caveman"!

When the month is up, Mr. McMahon calls you into his office in Connecticut.

"I'll be honest, I wasn't expecting this Caveman thing," he says. "But there's something there. I have a hunch—they may like you here in the states, but I think they'll really love Kid Caveman in Japan. I'm going to extend your contract."

You're a little bit disappointed about leaving the US, but going to Japan is kind of exciting. You know that a lot of Superstars have spent time working in Japan. Besides, it's better than being fired.

Mr. McMahon, as usual, is right. You're a huge sensation in Japan. You can't walk down the streets of Tokyo without being mobbed by fans. One night, you get a text message from Chris Jericho: *You proved me wrong, rookie. I'm impressed!*

## THE END

CONTINUED FROM PAGE 34

Mark Henry charges after you, and you suddenly realize that he just tossed The Miz over the ropes—what will he do to you? You quickly run to the corner and tag The Miz.

It's a good move. The Miz is steamed about being tossed out of the ring, and he takes it out on Mark Henry.

*Bam! Bam! Bam!* The Miz attacks swiftly with a barrage of punches. When Mark Henry tries to tag MVP, The Miz holds him back. He slams Henry with another punch. Then he climbs to the second rope and springboards off, knocking down Mark Henry with a clothesline.

MVP stretches his arm as far as it will go, but he can't reach. It's too late, anyway. The Miz pins Mark Henry. You've won the match!

Even though you didn't do much, it still feels great. The Miz grabs your hand and raises it in the air. The crowd boos, but you don't care. You're one step closer to the Royal Rumble.

"Don't try to be a hero," The Miz tells you back

in the locker room. "I know you're new at this. I can take most of these guys on my own. If I tell you to tag me, then tag me."

You nod. The Miz is in total control, but you're cool with that. If that's what it takes to win, you'll do it.

Your next match is against CM Punk and Luke Gallows. The two bearded wrestlers are as hungry for the championship as you are. It won't be an easy match.

The Miz and CM Punk start out in the ring first. Things look good early on. Punk is on the offensive, but The Miz turns all of his moves against him. When Punk jumps up and tries to take down The Miz with a bicycle kick, The Miz grabs him by his legs and swings him around.

*Whack!* Punk smacks into the ref, who slams onto the mat. The ref is out cold!

Gallows doesn't waste any time. He runs into the ring to help his teammate, even though it's an illegal move. But the ref isn't in any shape to stop him.

Your first instinct is to jump in the ring to help The Miz. Two against one isn't fair. Then you remember what The Miz told you: "Don't be a hero."

Maybe you should leave him alone to take down Punk and Gallows by himself. Besides, it's against the rules. If the ref comes to and catches you, you'll be disqualified.

If you jump into the ring and join the brawl, go to page 44.

If you decide to play by the rules and stay in your corner, go to page 53.

CONTINUED FROM PAGE 93

You decide to hit Tyson Kidd with a powerful side kick, hoping it will send him spiraling over the top rope. But he sees you out of the corner of his eye and grabs your leg.

It isn't good. Kidd uses your own momentum against you and whips your leg to the side. You lose your balance, falling back against the rope. Before you can recover, Kidd pushes you right out of the ring!

You jump to your feet, shaking your head. You're disappointed in yourself. You made it so far and then lost it all because of one bad decision.

## THE END

You decide to finish your business with Cody Rhodes first. Big Show is still into it with Mark Henry. When Evan enters the ring, he spends some time sizing up the situation.

Cody jumps up to deliver a dropkick to your chest. At the same moment, Mark Henry shoves Big Show, sending him staggering backward.

You push Cody as hard as you can. He flies back, slamming into Big Show. The angry giant frowns when he turns and sees that Cody has hit him. Before Cody can react, Big Show picks him up and tosses him over the top rope.

It worked! Now you just have to take care of Evan Bourne. But then Ted DiBiase enters the arena. He looks angry when he sees his former partner, Cody, sprawled on the floor.

That gives you an idea. "He did it!" you cry, pointing at Evan.

Angry, Ted chases after Evan to avenge his fallen partner. Once again, you've got a chance to rest for a few seconds.

You anxiously wait for the next Superstar to enter the ring. But after ninety seconds go by, you don't see anyone. What's happening?

Suddenly, you feel a hand around your ankle. It's Hornswoggle!

The tiny tough guy has slid into the ring without anyone noticing. He's got a strong grip, and he tries to pull you out of the ring with him. You grab onto the rope, struggling to hold on.

You call on your inner strength to break free of Hornswoggle's grasp. Then you reach for him and lift him over your head.

"So long, Hornswoggle!" you say, tossing him over the ropes.

You feel great. He's the first Superstar you've eliminated on your own!

When you turn back to the ring, you see that a lot has gone on while you were busy with Hornswoggle. Mark Henry and Big Show are still locked in battle, but Ted DiBiase and Evan Bourne are both out. R-Truth and Goldust have both entered the ring, and R-Truth has Goldust in a face lock. Then he falls, slamming Goldust into the mat.

You run up and grab Goldust's legs, nodding to R-Truth. Together, you get Goldust out of the ring.

Then R-Truth comes after you!

**If you use your corkscrew frog splash now, go to page 36.**

**If you try a safer move, go to page 61.**

CONTINUED FROM PAGE 39

The energy inside the ring completely changes. Everyone knows what's at stake—the ultimate prize. The winner of the Royal Rumble will see his reputation skyrocket and earn bragging rights for the rest of his career.

A free-for-all erupts onstage as everyone attacks one another. You get right into the fray, slamming Jack Swagger with an elbow drop. Rey Mysterio flies off the ropes and brings down Kofi Kingston. Chris Jericho pins you to the mat facedown and twists your legs behind you. The pain is excruciating.

Then Jack Swagger decides to go after Jericho, which is a bad move. Jericho picks him up and forces him over the side. At the same time, Rey Mysterio climbs the ropes again, but Kofi Kingston stops him this time, jumping to his feet and shoving Rey over the side.

Chris Jericho lunges for you again, but you do a backflip, ending up on the other side of the ring. Seeing that Jericho is distracted, Kofi quickly climbs the ropes and dives off, colliding into Jericho and knocking him down.

You run to Jericho's fallen body and you and Kofi work together to oust him from the ring. The crowd goes wild. You and Kofi face each other and slowly back away.

It's just you and Kofi left. You feel like you're dreaming. A few weeks ago you were wrestling in a high school gym, and now you're in the ring with an amazing Superstar, battling to win the Royal Rumble!

You're exhausted, but at least you know Kofi's been in the ring a long time, too. You just need to figure out your next . . .

*Bam!* Kofi launches himself off the rope behind him and slams into you, knocking you to the ground. Then he kneels on top of you and starts assaulting you with punches.

You muster every bit of strength you can and push him off you with a mighty shove. Then you kick him square in the chest, sending him reeling backward.

It's your move now, but you've got to think fast. Will you climb the ropes and attack from above, or go for a powerful move like a bodyslam to take Kofi out once and for all?

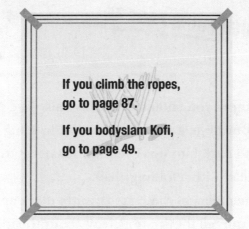

If you climb the ropes,
go to page 87.

If you bodyslam Kofi,
go to page 49.

You know you should probably talk The Miz out of the idea. But he just stood up for you in a big way—and you want to back him up. Even if it means getting bashed over the head with a folding chair.

The members of the Hart Dynasty don't answer right away. You can tell they're not crazy about the idea, either.

"What's it gonna be?" you ask. "Or are you afraid of getting beaten by a kindergartner?"

"It's on!" David Hart Smith says, his eyes blazing.

Mr. McMahon approves the idea for the match and sets up the rules. A golden ticket will be suspended from the ceiling, hanging a few feet above a ladder. The tag team to get the ticket will use it to face Morrison and MVP at the Royal Rumble. Tables and chairs set up around the ring can be used as legal weapons during the match.

The night of the Tables, Ladders & Chairs Match arrives, and you're more nervous than you've ever been. The tables and chairs around the ring look heavy and dangerous.

You start the match like a regular tag team match. The Miz and Smith start out in the ring, and you and

Kidd wait to be tagged. The Miz and Smith both go for the ladder. Smith gets to it first, and instead of climbing it, he picks it up and smacks The Miz right across the back.

The match goes on and on. The Miz smacks Smith with a folding chair. He retaliates by picking up The Miz and slamming him down on a table, breaking it. You jump in and try to set up the ladder again, but Kidd comes after you when you're halfway up. He tosses you off, and you go flying out of the ring, crashing into a pile of folding chairs.

In the end, Natalya ends up grabbing the golden ticket while the ref is knocked out. You've lost your chance to compete in the Royal Rumble!

You're devastated. But The Miz isn't that upset.

"Sometimes you win, and sometimes you lose," he says. "You did great out there. I'm proud to have you as my partner."

"Thanks," you say, and you feel better. Having a Superstar like The Miz say that is really awesome.

"Let's see what happens at the Royal Rumble," he says. "We'll challenge whoever wins the championship."

You smile. "Great idea!"

## THE END

CONTINUED FROM PAGE 57

Drew McIntyre is an arrogant 6'5" Scotsman who believes that he is the "Chosen One" picked by Mr. McMahon to save WWE. You charge at him, even though you're not sure how you're going to take him down.

You try to lift him up and bodyslam him, but McIntyre is stronger than you right now. He picks you up around the midsection and performs one of his most punishing moves, the spike piledriver.

The move rocks your world. You're helpless to fight back. McIntyre tosses you over the ropes like he's throwing out the garbage, and you hit the hard arena floor below with a thud.

As you're walking back to the locker room, you pass John Cena. He nods at you.

"Nice job for a rookie," he says.

You feel a little better. You didn't win, but you got a compliment from one of the greatest Superstars of all time!

**THE END**

CONTINUED FROM PAGE 83

You decide to go with your strength and try to finish off Kofi from the air. But in WWE, nothing is ever predictable. Right before you dive, you feel a hand on your shoulder.

Startled, you look behind you to see Hornswoggle standing on a ladder! The leprechaun has returned to get his revenge. He pulls you backward, and you, Hornswoggle, and the ladder go crashing to the ground.

"Kofi Kingston wins the Royal Rumble!" Jerry Lawler cries.

Hornswoggle runs away before you can take your anger out on him. You can't believe you lost! The crowd is cheering for Kofi as he does a victory lap around the ring.

Then it hits you—losing to a Superstar like Kofi Kingston is a real honor. And you lasted a long time in the ring. You're going to get respect for that, even though you didn't win.

"There's always next year!" you say.

## THE END

"Evan Bourne, I want you!" you say, pointing at him.

Evan grins and climbs to the top rope. Then it hits you—high-flying moves can be dangerous in the Royal Rumble.

You charge at Evan with all your might and push him over the top rope. He tries to hold on, but he can't, and slams onto the floor below. You've eliminated him!

You pump your first in the air. You're doing great! While you're distracted, Cody Rhodes slams into you from behind. The two of you start pummeling each other on the mat.

Before you know it, another Superstar enters the ring. You glance up and see Ted DiBiase standing over you. That's bad news.

Like Cody, Ted is the son of a WWE legend. The two Superstars were tag team partners. The Royal Rumble might be every man for himself, but when tag teams end up in the ring together, all bets are off.

Ted grabs your arms. Cody grabs your ankles.

They start to swing you back and forth. You try to break free, but these guys are strong.

They count together, "One, two, three!"

Then they toss you over the side like a sack of potatoes. You slam into the announcers' table, right in front of Jerry Lawler and Michael Cole.

"And Johnny Fresh is out of the Rumble!" Jerry cries.

You pick yourself up and dust yourself off. You didn't make it to the end of the Rumble, but that's okay. It was awesome just to be in the ring with some of your favorite Superstars!

## THE END

You're about to pick up the chair when you realize something—hitting someone with a chair while the ref is out is a bad guy move. If you do it, you could risk the whole good cop/bad cop thing you and The Miz have going.

You get back in your corner and hope that somehow The Miz can tag you. But Morrison's in control now. He lifts The Miz up off the ring and stands side-by-side with him, clamping an elbow around his neck. You gasp. Morrison's about to perform a finishing move—his Moonlight Drive!

*Bam!* You cringe as The Miz makes contact with the mat. It's all over. The ref is back in the ring now, and he counts out The Miz. Morrison and R-Truth win the match!

You rush into the ring to make sure The Miz is okay. He looks a little dazed, but he's fine.

"Sorry, man," you say. "I was going to hit Morrison with a chair, but I didn't want to ruin my good guy image, you know?"

"It's okay," The Miz says, and his voice is scratchy.

"I'm glad you didn't. I'm the one who does the bad guy stuff around here."

So you don't win the championship, but you and The Miz remain a popular tag team. Within a few months, WWE puts out a T-shirt of you and The Miz with your picture on a white background on one side and his picture against a black background on the other side. It's really cool. All in all, you're pretty happy with the choices you've made.

## THE END

CONTINUED FROM PAGE 11

Even though the ref is still down, you decide to get back in the ring and see what happens. You may be a bad guy, but you don't want to be known as a coward.

"Looks like Johnny Fresh is feeling *refreshed* from his time outside the ring," Lawler quips from the announcers' table.

In the ring, Matt Hardy bounces off the corner rope and knocks down Kofi with a clothesline. Cena has found a more worthy opponent than you in Sheamus and the two men are trading punches. Tyson Kidd, part of the Hart Dynasty and a great technical wrestler, jumps into the ring and goes right for you.

He hits you in the chest with a powerful roundhouse kick. It knocks the wind out of you, but you recover and grip him around the shoulders. Then you push him against the ropes, hoping he'll tumble to the other side.

Chris Masters enters the ring next. "The Masterpiece" is known for his masterful physique, as well as his memorable finishing move, the Master Lock. It's a full nelson. Masters pushes his opponents' heads forward with intense pressure. The move has brought many Superstars to their knees.

Masters must have some beef with Tyson Kidd because he pulls you off him and grabs the other wrestler by the shoulders. Now Masters has his back to you—you can attack him, and he won't even know it's coming.

**If you hit him with a side kick, go to page 77.**

**If you try a half nelson slam, go to page 19.**

"Uh, Miz," you say. "I don't think I can compete in a Tables, Ladders & Chairs Match right now. I just don't have enough experience."

The members of the Hart Dynasty start to laugh.

"Ha! Looks like your little friend is afraid of some furniture, Miz," taunts Tyson Kidd. But you notice he seems a little relieved.

"We don't need to prove anything," Smith adds. "See you in the ring."

Smith, Kidd, and Natalya walk away.

"Sorry," you tell The Miz. "I didn't mean to chicken out."

"Well, you're probably right," The Miz says. "A Tables, Ladders & Chairs Match wasn't a great idea. I guess I got carried away. Those losers made me so angry!"

"Then let's use that in the ring," you say.

The Miz nods. "Right!"

Mr. McMahon schedules the match for *Monday Night Raw*. By now, you and The Miz have your costumes down. You're wearing white shorts and white wrestling boots. They're embroidered with gold angel wings. The Miz is wearing black shorts and black boots with a red pitchfork embroidered on each one.

The members of the Hart Dynasty are wearing their signature hot-pink and black costumes. You see them as you enter the backstage waiting area.

"Good luck," Natalya says. "You're gonna need it!"

Then the announcer's voice blares through the stadium.

"The following contest is a tag team match. The winner will move on to face the Unified WWE Tag Team Champions at the Royal Rumble!"

The crowd goes wild. You and The Miz enter the ring first, followed by the Hart Dynasty. An electric feeling courses through your body. Something tells you that you and The Miz are going to win.

By now you've got your good cop/bad cop routine perfectly set. The Miz breaks the rules, and you try to stick to them. When Tyson Kidd pins your arms behind your back, The Miz sneaks up behind him and pulls him away from you when the ref isn't looking. When Natalya distracts the ref so that Kidd and Smith can double-team The Miz, you clothesline her from behind.

In the end, Smith twists your legs with an incredibly painful sharpshooter. But you don't tap out.

Instead, you manage to pull yourself down the ring using the ropes, little by little, until you tag The Miz. He jumps in and pins a stunned Smith before he knows what's hit him.

You jump up and let out a whoop. You're going to the Royal Rumble!

Go to page 64.